THE BLOODY MOON OF PETERS LIFE

GURU PRASAD SWAIN

CHAPTER 1

PETERS LIFE

Long, Long Ago There Was A Boy Named Peter. He Was A Very Naughty Child. He Always Pranks People, Who Are Walking, Talking, Standing. He Had A Disorder Named 'Munchausen' Or 'Paranoid Personality Disorder'. This Is A Type of Disease in Which Someone Tries to Get Attention or Sympathy. They Also Think That Others Are Always Trying Them to Demean, Harm or Threaten Them. His Mother, Father and His Friends Know About His Disorder. If He Is Out of Control His Friends Know How to Handle Him. One Day Peter Was Playing with Is Friends So He Decided to Climb Up in The Tree and Feel Like A King and Give Orders to His Friends. After Following His Orders His Friends Decided to Prank Him, So His Friends Ran and Hidden Behind the Tree. Peter Called His Friends but Nobody Came. After Some Time Peter Got Panicked and He Fell Down from The Tree. His Friends Ran Towards Him. Peter Was Losing Blood. He Was Rushed to The Hospital. Doctor Said That He Will Not Be Able to Walk. After Listening This Peter Was Sad. He Thought That My Disorder Made Me Do This. He Told His Mother About This. His Mother Said 'Don't Worry About It, You Will Be Fine Soon, My Child' After That He Thought That He Would Have Control on Himself. He Always Sits Near the Window and Watches His Friends Playing and Having Fun. His Mother Was Very Sad Seeing His Child Sitting Near the Window and Watching. Days and Days Passed Away. One Day Peter's Mother Was Shocked After Seeing His Child Standing on His Own Legs. Her Eyes Filled with Tears, And Hugged Peter. His Friends Were Very Happy After Seeing Him After So Long Time. After Some Times His Friends Noticed That He Was Not Pranking the People Who Were Standing, Talking and Walking, But Greeting Them. Peter's Friend Told Him That Your

Disorder Has Been Gone, You Are Greeting People, Rather Than Pranking Them. After Noticing It He Was Happy. One Day He Was Walking Along A Street Singing Song in His Mind. He Suddenly Noticed A Strange Man with A Strange Bag with Him. He Suddenly Rushed to Him and Asking Him That You Are New to This Town, But There Was No Replay from Him. So, He Started Following Him. After He Travelled A Long Distance, The Man Stopped in A Dense Jungle Were, He Opened His Strange Bag and Took A Strange Stick Out of His Bag. It Was A Long Stick with Two Wings' on It. He Was Looking at Him So Seriously but He Stepped on A Stick. This Created A Sound Which Attracted the Attention of The Strange Man. The Boy Got Scared and He Rushed Behind the Bushes. The Strange Man Came to The Place Where the Boy Was Hiding. The Boy Was Little Scared Because He Was 5 Meters Away from The Spot Where He Stepped on The Stick. The Boy Was Thinking That 'How This Strange Man Know My Location?' He Was Puzzled. The Man Started Searching Peter, But He Slowly, Slowly Walked Away from The Eyes of The Stranger. The Stranger Was Finding Him For 40 Min. He Was Tired and Bored; He Was Feeling Sleepy Too. So, The Stranger Decided to Go and Sit Under A Tree and Have Some Rest. After Some Time Peter Arrived with His Friends. Peter Said That 'Look He Is A Strange Man Who Can Locate Anyone's Position' His Friends Were Shocked. His Friends Said to Run Away or We Will Be in A Big Trouble, But Little That They Knower That the Strange Man Was Acting of Sleeping. When Peter and His Friends Were Going Home, They Felt A Strange Feeling That Somoni Was Watching Them from The Tree. They Were Little Scared About That Feeling. They Went Home. Peter and His Family Were Having Lunch, But Peter Was Little Scared. His Mother Asked 'What Happened to You Dear. You Are Looking Little Scared. Is There Any Problem, Tell Me I Am Your Mother', So Peter Started Telling the Whole Incident to His Mother and Father? Both Were Shocked After Listening This, But Father Said the He Is Jacking with Us, Don't Worry About It, But Mother Didn't Obey the Words of The Father, She Was Deeply Thinking About the Incidence. It Was Too Late

Night and Mother and Father Were Tired So They Went to Sleep. Peter on That Side Was Still Thinking About That Stick, The Strange Man, His Strange Bag, His Ability of Knowing the Location of The Person and The Strange Feeling. He Was Not Able to Sleep That Night. It Was A Beautiful Morning but A Bad Morning for Peter and His Friends Because This Was the Day When Peter and His Friends Will Meet the Strange Man Face to Face, But the Strange Man Will Be in A Disguise and Will Meet Peter in A Coffee Shop Today. Peter Was Not Knowing About This but It Was Planned by The STRANGE MAN.

**TO BE CONTINUED IN CHAPTER -2 ....*

<u>CHAPTER 2</u>

<u>THE STRANGE MAN</u>

THE DAY HAS ARRIVED WHEN I HAVE TO MEET MY SWEET FRIEND PETER. THE STRANGE MAN NAME IS 'MARK'. MARK IS A PERSON WITH SOME SPECIAL ABILITY TO KNOW THE LOCATION AND DISGUISE HIMSELF. THE STRANGE STICK IN HIS BAG WAS HELPING HIM TO DISGUISE. MARK WAS A SIMPLE MAN DOING FARMING. ONE DAY HE WAS JUST WALKING ON THE STREET AND SUDDENLY NOTICED A STRANGE BAG LYING ON THE ROAD. AT FIRST HE IGNORED IT BUT HIS MIND WAS SAYING HIM TO PICK IT UP. AFTER HE TOOK THAT BAG TO HOME, HE FOUND A STRANGE STICK, IT WAS A LONG STICK HAVING TWO WINGS ON IT. AT FIRST HE THOUGHT THAT IT WAS A TOY BUT, LITTLE DOES HE KNOW THAT, THIS ORDANIRY STICK CAN HELP HIM DISGUISE AND HAVE THE ABILITY TO KNOW ANYONES LOCATION. HE STARTED SEARCHING THE STRANGE BAG MORE DEEPLY, AND FOUND A LETTER IN WHICH IT WAS

THE STRANGR STICK

AND

ITS MESTARY

THE PERSON WHO WILL FIND THIS STICK IS THE OWNER OF THIS MAGICAL STICK. THIS STICK HAS THE ABILITY TO HELP YOU DISGUISE AND KNOW THE LOCATION OF ANYONE. TO USE THIS STICK, YOU HAVE TO BE ALONE IN A DENCE JUNGLE WHERE NO ONE CAN SEE YOU.IF ANYONE SEES AND IS NEAR 4METERS THIS WILL NOT WORK.

THANKYOU FOR READING THIS LETTER HOPE YOU WILL USE THIS STICK!

WRITTEN THAT..........

AFTER READING THIS, FIRST HE WAS THINKING SOMEONE WAS JOCKING. SO, HE DECIDED TO TRY IT OUT. HE LEFT IS HOME AND STARTED WALKING TO THE DENCE FOREST. ON HIS WAY HE WAS PASSING THROUGH A TOWN NAMED 'GREEN HEVEN' WHERE PETER AND HIS FRIENDS WERE LIVING. MARK STARTED WALKING THROUGH THE TOWN WHILE PETER WAS WALKING ON THE STREET SINGING SONG IN HIS MIND. MARK PASSED PETER. PETER SAW MARK AND CALLED HIM. HE GREATED MARK, BUT MARK WAS IN A HURRY SO HE DIDN'T REPLAY AND LEFT

WITHOUT REPLYING TO PETER. FROM THAT INCEDENCE PETER STARTED FOLLOWING MARK. THEY BOTH HAD ARRIVED IN A DENCE JUNGLE. PETER WAS BEHIND THE BUSHES AND 5 METERS AWAY FROM MARK. MARK TOOK OUT HIS STICK AND STARTED SAYING SOMETHING TO THE STICK. ON THAT TIME PETER STEPPED ON A STICK. AS THE SOUND REACHED TO MARK THE STICK SUDDENLY STARTED WORKING. THE STICK WAS GIVING MARK INSTRUCTIONS THAT WHERE WAS PETER. PETER RAN TO THE OTHER SIDE BUT STILL MARK FOUND THE LOCATION, SO PETER WAS SCARED ABOUT THAT AND DECIDED TO RUN AWAY. FROM THAT TIME MARK NEWED THAT THIS STICK IS NOT ORDANIRY BUT SOMETHING SPECIAL THAT NO ONE KNOWS. AFTER SOMETIME THE STICK WAS GIVING INSTRUCTIONS THAT 'YOU SHOULD GO UNDER A TREE AND DO AN ACTING OF SLEEPING' MARK OBEYED THE ORDERS AND WENT UNDER A TREE AND ACTED AS IF HE WAS A SLEEP. AFTER SOMETIME PETER ARRIVED WITH HIS FRIENDS, AND ON THAT MOMENT, MARK HAD GOT THE ABILITY TO DISGUISE HIMSELF. MARK WAS LISTNING THERE TALKS VERY CAREFULLY. WHEN PETER AND HIS FRIENDS LEFT, MARK STARTED FOLLOWING THEM AND CLIMBED ON A TREE AND STARTED WATCHING THEM. MARK STARTED PLANNING THAT HOW SHOULD I MEET MY LITTLE FRIEND PETER AND HIS INNOCENT FRIENDS WHICH ARE INVOLVED IN MY SECRET STICK. IT TOOK MARK NEARLY 2 HOURS TO PLAN. HE DECIDED THAT FIRST HE WILL DISGUISE HIMSELF AS A SHOPKEEPER OF THE COFFEE SHOP AND GO HIS HOUSE AND INVITE HIM. THEN I WILL BECOME AN ORDANIRY MAN WHICH WERE IN THE TOWN, AND I WILL REQUEST HIM TO LET ME MEET YOUR FRIENDS AND FAMILY. THEN I WILL VANISH HIM HIS FRIENDS AND FAMILY, SO THAT NO ONE KNOWS ABOUT ME AND MY STRANGE STICK. TO BE CONTINUED ......

CHAPTER-3

THE COFFEE SHOP

THE DAY HAS CAME WHEN I HAVE TO MEET MY LITTLE FRIEND PETER. IT WAS THE DAY OF SUNDAY. ACCORDING TO HIS PLAN HE HAD TO GO TO HIS HOME AT 9.00 AM TO INVITE HIM, HIS FAMILY AND FRIENDS TO THE COFFEE SHOP. SO, HE WENT TO THE FOREST DISGUISED HIMSELF AND CAME TO PETERS HOUSE. HE RANG THE DOORBELL. TRING, TRING, THE MOTHER OPENED THE DOOR AND ASKED 'WHO ARE YOU?' MARK REPLIED THAT I AM THE SHOPKEEPER OF THE COFFEE SHOP. I AM INVITING YOU TO OUR COFFEE SHOP TO HAVE SOME TASTY COFFEE. YOU CAN ALSO INVITE YOUR FRIENDS TO MY SHOP. I WILL BE HAPPY IF YOU WILL COME TO MY SHOP. AFTER SOME TIME PETER ARRIVED AT THE COFFEE SHOP. MARK WAS VERY HAPPY TO SEE HIM AND WAS THINKING THAT, EVERYTHING IS GOING ACCORDING TO MY PLAN. AS PETER AND HIS FRIENDS ARRIVED THE AGAIN FELT A STRANGE FEELING THE SOMETHING IS GOING WRONG. PETER SAT DOWN NEAR A MAN WHO WAS JUST LOOKING LIKE A HOME TOWN MAN. PETER DIDN'T FOUND HIM SUSPICEOUS, BUT LITTLE THAT HE KNOWS THAT ORDANIRY MAN WHO WAS SITTING NEAR PETER WAS MARK. WHO HAS DISGUISED HIMSELF AS AN ORDANIRY MAN OF THE HOME TOWN, BOTH WERE TALKING AND HAVING FUN? AFTER THIS THEY STARTED TELLING THEIR OLDER MEMORIES TO EACH OTHER AND REACTED ON IT. PETERS OLD MEMORIES TO BE CONTINUED......

CHAPTER 4

THE PHOTOGRAPH

A FEW MONTHS AGO, A FRIEND OF MINE, WHO IS AN UP-AND-COMING NATURE PHOTOGRAPHER, DECIDED TO

*SPEND A DAY AND NIGHT ALONE IN THE WOODS OUTSIDE OF OUR TOWN. HE WANTED TO GET PHOTOS OF THE WOODS AND WILDLIFE AS NATURALLY AS HE COULD FOR HIS PORTFOLIO. HE WASN'T AFRAID OF BEING ALONE, AS HE HAD CAMPED BY HERSELF MANY TIMES BEFORE. HE SAT UP A TENT IN THE MIDDLE OF A SMALL CLEARING AND SPENT THE DAYS BY TAKING PICTURES. SHE FILLED UP FOUR ROLLS OF FILM ON THAT TRIP, BUT SOMETHING WAS STRANGE ABOUT THEM. WHAT HE SAW IN THOSE PICTURES HAS STAYED WITH HIM, AND HE IS STILL TRYING TO RECOVER FROM THE TRAUMA THE HAVE CAUSED HIM. ALMOST EVERY PICTURE WAS ACCOUNTED FOR, SAVE FOR ONE PICTUREIN EACH ROLL OF FILM. THESE PICTURES WERE OF HIM, ASLEEP IN HER TENT IN THE MIDDLE OF THE NIGHT. THEY WERE SCARED AFTER SEEING THIS ROLL OF FILM AND KNOWED THAT WHY CAN HE COME BACK FROM HIS TRAUMA.
PETERS OLD*

<u>CHAPTER 5</u>

<u>MY MOM WASN'T MAKING IT UP AFTER * ALL*</u>

SO, A WHILE BACK MY MOM LIVED IN THIS HOUSE ON BRINDLEY MOUNTAIN(ALABAMA). THE LANDLORD TO THE PLACE WAS SUPER ANAL ABOUT MAKING SURE THEY DID NO REMODELING OR REPAIRS... HE WANTED NOTHING CHANGED. IT WAS ODD TO SAY THE LEAST. AFTER A WHILE MY MOM AND HER BF STARTED SAYING THEY THINKTHE PLACE WAS HAUNTED BY THE GHOST OF A SMALL GIRL. THEY SAID SOMETIMES THEY WOULD SEE THE SHADOW OF A GIRL WALK FROM ROOM TO ROOM. OR HEAR PLAYING IN THE BACK WHEN NOBODY WAS BACKTHERE, AND SOMETIMES IT SOUNDED LIKE A SMALL CHILD WAS SOBBING BUT COULDN'T TELL WHERE. ME BEING AN ATHEIST AT THE TIME, I KINDA BLEW IT

OFF. I WAS LIKE "YEAH...RIGHT...HAHA" SO ANYWAY. THIS WAS TOWARDS END OF ME AND EX'S RELATIONSHIP. WHEN WE SPLIT UP, I STARTEDLIVING WITH MY MOM UNTIL I GOT ON MY FEET. WE SHARED CUSTODY OF OUR DAUGHTER, ALEXIS, 50/50.SO ONE WEEK SHE'D STAY WITH ME UNTIL FRIDAY, AND THEN SHE'D GO TO MY EX'S UNTILTHE FOLLOWING FRIDAY, AND THEN SHE'D COME BACK WITH ME. SHE WAS ABOUT 2 GOING ON 3 AT THE TIME. IT WAS SUNDAY NIGHT AND I WAS ON THE COMPUTER. ITS PROBABLY LIKE 2 IN THE MORNING. I'M JUST SURFING MUSIC. THE COMPUTER DESK WAS IN THE KITCHEN FACING A WALL, AND ON THAT SAME WALL WAS THE DOORWAY THAT LED TO THE DENAND THE BEDROOMS, SO IF ANYONE CAME OUT OF BED TO GET SOMETHING FROM THE KITCHEN THEN THEY WOULD WALK RIGHT PASSED ME. ALEXIS WAS ALWAYS GETTING UP IN THE NIGHT AND GETTING INTO TROUBLE. SHE'D RAID THE FRIDGE OR KNOCK SOMETHING OVER WHILE CLIMBING UP ON SOMETHING. SHE LIKED TO GRT UP IN THE NIGHT AND RAID THE KITCHEN BECAUSE SHE KNEW EVERYONE WAS ASLEEP AND SHE COULD GET AWAY WITH IT. SO AS I SAID BEFORE, THIS NIGHT I HAPPENED TO BE UP AT 2 AM AT THE COMPUTER. I SEE ALEXIS SNEAK INTO THE KITCHEN WITH MY PERIPHERAL VISION AND SHE FROZE WHEN SHE SAW ME. AND JUST STOOD THERE. I DIDN'T LOOK AT HER OR PAY HER ATTENTION. I FIGURED SHE HAD SEEN ME... SHE KNOWS SHE'S CAUGHT, HOPEFULLY SHE WILL GO BACK TO BED AND GO TO SLEEP WITHOUT ME HAVING TO MAKE A BIG DEAL OF IT. SO SHE STANDS THERE FOR ABOUT 3 MIN, AND I CAN SEE HER WHOLE TIME BUT I MAKE A POINT NOT TO LOOK AT HER SO SHE WILL JUST GO BACK TO BED. SHE EVENTUALLY TURNS AND WALKS BACK TOWARDS THE BEDROOM. IT WAS DARK IN THE ROOM...BUT I COULD STILL SEE HER TURN AND LEAVE. EVERY THING WAS DEAD AND SILENT AFTER THAT. SO AFTER ABOUT 15 MIN, I GOT THAT

FEELING IN MY GUT THAT I NEED TO CHECK ON HER BECAUSE SHE'S PROBABALY UP TO NO GOOD... IN 15 MIN I SHOULD HAVE HEARD HER CLIMB BACK IN BED OR RUSTLE THROUGH TOYS. HEARING ABSOLUTELY NOTHING NORMALLY MENT SHE WAS TRYING TO BE QUITE FOR A REASON. EVERY PERENT GETS THAT SICK FEELING IN THEIR STOMACH WHEN THEIR KID IS UP TO NO GOOD, AND I GOT THAT FEELING SO I GOT UP TO CHECK ON HER. I STOOD UP AND WALKED INTO THE NEXT ROOM THAT LED TO THE BEDROOMS. AND IT WAS PITCH BLACK... COULDN'T SEE A THING. AND THAT'S WHEN IT HIT ME... ALEXIS WAS WITH MY EX THAT NIGHT, NOT WITH ME. I HAD BEEN USED TO HER BEING THERE ALL WEEK THAT IT JUST SLIPPED MY MIND. SO, THE GIRL I SAW, WASN'T HER ... PETERS OLD STORIES TO BE CONTINUED ......

CHAPTER 6

A CURIOUS* *WARNING*

LAST NIGHT, AS I WAS SITTING IN MY LIVING ROOM AND WATCHING A LITTLE TV BEFORE BED, I HEARD A STRANGE NOISE. IT WAS A SLOW, DRAWN OUT SCRAPING ACROSS THE HARDWOOD FLOOR. CONFUSED, I SEARCHED FOR THE SOURCE OF THE SOUND; AND I FOUND IT IMMEDIATELY. SOMEONE HAD A SLIPPED A SMALL, FOLDED NOTE UNDER THE DOOR. "WHAT THE HELL?" MORE CURIOUS THAN ANYTHING, I APPROACHED THE NOTE SLOWLY. I KNELT DOWN CAUTIOUSLY AND PICKED UP THE STRANGE PAPER. ON IT WERE ONLY FIVE WORDS, SCRAWLED ON IT A CRUDE, MESSY FASHION: "GET OUT. HE IS COMING." I DIDN'T PAUSE TO CONSIDER THE MEANING OF THE NOTE, HOWEVER, AS I IMMEDIATELY REALIZED THERE WAS SOMETHING VERY, VERY WRONG WITH THIS SITUATION: THE NOTE HAD COME FROM

UNDER THE CLOSET DOOR. HE WAS VERY, VERY SCARED AFTER THIS INCIDENCE AND W

HE FELT LEAVING ITS HOUSE AND GO TO HIS GRANDMAS HOUSE.... PETERS OLD STORIED TO BE CONTINUED.....................

<u>CHAPTER 7</u>

<u>GIRL in THE *PHOTOGRAPH*</u>

ONE SCHOOL DAY, PETER AND HIS FRIENDS NAMED TOM, MARK AND SOFIA WERE SITTING IN CLASS AND DOING MATH. IT WAS SIX MORE MINUTIES UNTIL AFTER SCHOOL, AS HE WAS DOING HIS HOMEWORK. SOMETHING CAUGHT HIS EYE. HIS DESK WAS NEXT TO THE WINDOW. HE LOOKED OUTSIDE ON THE GRASS. IT LOOKED LIKE A PICTURE. WHEN SCHOOL WAS OVER, HE RAN TO THE SPOT WHERE HE SAW IT, HE RAN FAST SO THAT NO ONE ELSE COULD GRAB IT. HE PICKED IT UP AND SMILED. IT HAD A PICTURE OF THE MOST BEAUTIFUL GIRL HE HAD EVER SEEN. SHE HAD A DRESS WITH LIGHTS ON AND RED SHOES AND HER HAND WAS FORMED INTO A PEACE SIGN. SHE WAS SO BEAUTIFUL HE WANTED TO MEET HER, SO HE RAN AT OVER THE SCHOOL AND ASKED EVERYONE IF THEY KNOW HER OR HAVE EVER SEEN HER BEFORE, BUT EVERYONE HE ASKED SAID "NO" HE WAS TRYING VERY HARD TO FIND HER. WHEN HE WAS HOME, HE ASKED HIS OLDER SISTER IF SHE KNOW THE GIRL, BUT UNFORTUNATELY, SHE ALSO SAID "NO" IT WAS VERY LATE, SO PETER WALKED UP THE STAIRS, PLACED THE PICTURE ON HIS BEDSIDE TABLE AND WENT TO SLEEP. IN THE MIDDLE OF THE NIGHT PETER WAS AWAKENED BY A TAP ON HIS WINDOW. IT WAS LIKE NAIL TAPPING. HE GOT SCARED, AFTER THE TAPPING HE HEARD A GIGGLE. HE SAW A SHADOW NEAR HIS WINDOW, SO HE GOT OUT OF HIS BED, WALKED TOWARDS THE WINDOW, OPENED

IT UP AND FOLLOWED THE GIGGLING, BY THE TIME HE REACHED IT, IT WAS GONE. THE NEXT DAY AGAIN HE ASKED HIS NEIGHBOURS IF THEY KNEW HER. EVERYBODY SAID, "SORRY, NO" WHEN HIS MOTHER CAME HOME, HE EVEN ASKED HER IF SHE KNEW HER. SHE SAID "NO" HE WENT TO HIS ROOM, PLACED THE PICTURE ON HIS DESK AND FELL ASLEEP. ONCE AGAIN, HE WAS AWAKENED BY A TAPPING. HE TOOK THE PICTURE AND FOLLOWED THE GIGGLING. HE WALKED ACROSS THE ROAD, WHEN SUDDENLY HE GOT HIT BY A CAR. HE WAS RUSHED TO THE HOSPITAL WITH THE PICTURE IN HIS HAND. THE DRIVER GOT VERY PANICKED AND SCARED. THE DRIVER WAS GIVEN THE PICTURE WHICH WAS WITH PETER. HE SAW A CUTE GIRL HOLIDING UP THREE FINGERS. THE DRIVER WAS VERY CONFUSED ABOUT THAT PICTURE OF THE GIRL. THE DRIVER TORE THE PICTURE AND THROWN THE PICTURE IN THE DUSTBIN.

CHAPTER 8 THE STATUE*

A FEWYEARS AGO, MY MOTHER AND FATHER DECIDED THEY NEEDED A BREAK, SO THEY WANTED TO HEAD OUT FOR A NIGHT ON THE TOWN. THEY CALLED THEIR MOST TRUSTED BABYSITTER. WHEN THE BABYSITTER ARRIVED, THE TWO CHILDERN WERE ALREADY FALT ASLEEP IN BEB. SO, THE BABYSITTER JUST GOT TO SIT AROUND AND MAKE SURE EVERYTHING WAS OKAY WITH THE CHILDERN. LATER THAT NIGHT, THE BABYSITTER GOT BORED AND WENT TO WATCH TV, BUT SHE COULDN'T WATCH IT DOWNSTAIRS BECAUSE THEY DID NOT HAVE CABLE DOWNSTAIRS. SO, SHE CALLED THEM AND ASKED THEM IF SHE COULD WATCH CABLE IN THE PARENT'S ROOM. THE PARENTS SAID IT WAS OK, BUT THE BABYSITTER HAD ONE FINAL REQUEST- SHE ASKED IF SHE COULD COVER UP THE STATUE OUTSIDE THE BEDROOM WINDOW WITH A BLANKET OR CLOTH,

BECAUSE IT MADE HER NERVOUS. THE PHONE LINE WAS SILENT FOR A MOMENT, AND THE FATHER WHO WAS TALKING TO THE BABYSITTER AT THE TIME SAID, "TAKE THE CHILDREN AND GET OUT OF THE HOUSE, WE DON'T OWN A STATUE." THE POLICE FOUND BOTH THE CHILDREN AND THE BABYSITTER SLUMPED IN POOLS OF THEIR OWN BIOOD WITHIN THREE MINUTES OF THE CALL. THE POLICE STARTED FINDING THE STATUE. IT TOOK THEM NEARLY 5 DAYS TO FIND THE STATUE BUT THEY COULDN'T FIND THE STATUE. THE STATUE WAS NOT FOUND. THIS WAS STILL A, UNKNOWN MESTRY ....

*Chapter 9

bloody moon

IT WAS A WONDERFUL DAY IN THE TOWN OF (ALABAMA) AND PETER AND KEVIN WERE OUT FOR A WALK IN THE MOUNTAINS ON THER LAST VACATION DAY. THE VIEW WAS EXTRODERNERY. MONA PLANTINGS TURNING THE OTHERWISE DRY LAND GREEN AND SMALL WHITE HOUSES FORMING TINY VILLAGES, EVERYTHING BATHING IN THE STRONG SUNLIGHT. AS THEY WALKED UPON AN OLD PATH WITH A HIGH CLIFF ON THE LEFT– HAND –SIDE THEY PASSED A YELLOW SIGN WITH SOME TEXT AND THE CLIFF PAINTED IN BLACK, BUT SINCE NEITHER OF THEM SPOKE SPANISH THEY THOUGHT NOTHING OF IT. THEY WALKED ON BY AND ENJOYED EACH OTHERS COMPANIES VERY MUCH, HOLDING HANDS AND TALKING ABOUT THEIR HOLIDAY. SUDDENLY KEVIN STOPPED AND CLAIMED THAT SHE HEARD A NOISE OF A ROCK FALLING DOWN FROM THE MOUNTAIN BESIDE THEM, BUT KEVIN ASSURED HER THAT IT WAS PERFECTLY OKAY FOR THEM TO CONTINUE THEIRWALK, SINCE HE WAS ENJOYING IT SO MUCH. JUST A SECOND AFTER HE SPOKE THOSE WORDS A LOUD NOISE SHAKE

THE GROUND AND BEFORE AND BEFORE THEY EVEN HAD TIME TO REACT, MASSIVE ROCKSWERE FLYING DOWN FROM THE CLIFF JUST BESIDE THEM. THEY THREW THEMSELVES AGAINST A BIG TREE NEXT TO THE PATH AS ROCKS KEPT FALLING DOWN AND DUST STARTED TO FILL THE AIR. THE HORRIBLE MOMENT SEEMEDTO LAST FOREVER... AT LAST IT STOPPED, AND EVERYTHING TURNED DEAD SILENCE. AFTER A FEW SECONDS, VOICE WAS HEARD SHOUTING: "KEVIN, ARE YOU OKAY? WHERE ARE YOU? IT WAS KEVIN OF COURSE. HE WAS LYING UNDER THE TREE, AND SEEMED TO BE SAFE AND SOUND DESPITE THE HORRIBLE INCIDENT. A FEW SECONDS WENT BY WITHOUT AN ANSWRE FROM PETER. HE STARTED PANICING AND SHOUTING, EVEN LOUDER AND MORE ANXIOUS THAN BEFORE. THEN SILENTLY, BUT STILL, A WAGE SOUND WAS HEARD. KEVIN JUMPED UP FROM THE PLACE HE WAS LYING ON AND STARTED TO LOOK AROUND. THERE, ON THE PATH, UNDER A PILE OF ROCKS HE SAW A RED THING BUT HE COULDN'T DISTINGUISH WHAT IT WAS. COMING CLOSER, HE SAW THAT KEVON WAS LYING THERE AND THAT THE RED WAS FROM HER T-SHIRT WHICH SHE WORE THAT KEVIN WAS LYING THERE AND THAT BIGGEST ROCK ON TOP AND STARTED TO PUSH, AT FIRST IT WAS ALL STILL WHICH MADE PETER AGAIN TO PANIC. WITH ALL HIS FORCE HE PUSHED ONCE AGAIN AND NOW IT SLOWLY STARTED TO MOVE AND FINALLY, AFTER AN HEROIC EFFORT THE ROCK SLID OFF AND KEVIN COULD GET LOOSE. SHE MIRACULOUSLY WAS ALSO WITHOUT ANY SEVERE INJURIES AND HUGGED PETER HARDER THAN EVER BEFORE, AND THEY AGREED THAT THEY WON'T IGNORE SIGNS THEY DON'T UNDERSTAND EVER AGAIN. THEY HAD THOUGHT THAT THEY WILL FIND IT OUT, BUT THEY DIDN'T FOUND IT. IT WAS DIFFICULT AND THEY DIDN'T FOUND IT AND IT WAS A, UNKNOWN MYSTERY WHICH WAS NOT FOUND. PETERS OLD STORIES CONTINUED...

CHAPTER 10

THE UNKNOWN *BARGAIN*

There's A Small Building in The Town Called 'Padraic Winnows by And Co.' In the Industrial District of Alabama, United States. Most of The Time. Most of The Time, Its Doors Are Locked and The Windows Are Draped. However, On February 29TH Of Every Leap Year, There Will Be A Small Plastic Container Outside the Front Door Containing Business Cards. On the Front of The Card It Says in Large Capital Letters. 'Padraic Winnows by And Co. United States Munchausen Specialists''. On the Back, In the Nearly Illegibly Small Type It Says "The Blood of The Innocent". Any Night After Midnight One Can Come to Padraic Winnows and Co. And Slide Their Card Through the Door, And the Door Will Instantly Unlock. Inside There Is an Empty Room with White Walls No Light Reaches This Room, Except For A Small Silver from The Other End of The Room. When You Approach This Room, You Will Find That It Is Actually Another Door. When You Knock on It, A Voice Will Ask "What Makes A Man Become Exited?" And You Must Respond with The Phrase on The Back of The Card: "The Blood of The Innocent". The Door Will Open and You Will Come into Another Room, A Kind of Lounge. Inside It You Will Find Around 5-10 People, Depending on The Night, Sitting Around Smoking and Drinking Brandy, All in Late Edwardian Period Dress. There Is Absolutely No Conversation at All in This Room And, It Is Nearly Silent Except For The Phonograph Which Plays the Exact Same Record Over and Over, And Infinitum. If You Attempt to Speak to One of The Patrons, They Will Promptly Ignore You and Pretend as If You Were Not There.

CHAPTER- 11

THE WOODS

The air feels heavy with dust and it tickles the back of his throat. Awkwardly, he remembers and steps aside to let the other man in.

The buyer steps inside after the realtor and, like him, stops to take it all in. He scans the room, absorbing the old furniture, the layer of dust covering everything like a shroud. The dust in the air is heavy and gives his throat a dry tickle that makes him want to cough.

With a distracted nod to the realtor, he steps further into the house, feeling a momentary pang of regret for not taking his shoes off. "You are supposed to take your shoes off when you enter someone's home," he thinks. He looks around taking it all in.

"It's eerie how the house feels like the family just left it moments ago, like they are about to come back at any time. The house looks lived in, except for the thirty years of dust coating everything and the vague feeling of abandonment."

The mostly green cover of a comic book left laying open on the floor catches his eye. He picks up the comic book and looks at it, trying not to disturb too much of the dust clinging to it. It's unavoidable, his fingers rub smudges in the dust coating the old comic book. The Thing, an orange blocky comic book creation made of stone, part monster and all hero. On the cover, The Thing appears to be battling a many-armed green wall, the green arms surrounding him in a barrage of punching fists. Marvel Comics, The Thing issue #21 dated March 1985. The price on it is sixty cents.

The top front corner is curled from a boy's rough handling.

He puts it down with a frown, wondering if it's worth anything on the collectors' market. He can't take it, though. It belongs to the municipality, along with the property and its contents. At least until after the auction. He hopes the realtor didn't notice it.

"How often do realtors scoop up gems like this without anyone ever knowing?" he wonders.

The breath of the men betrayed their nature. They wore the right faces, but those yellow sulphurous exhalations belonged to no mortal. In black suits, with dark glasses, they stood with their arms folded looking in on the girl lying in the hospital bed. The monitor blipped in time with her heartbeat and their chests rose and fell with the same rhythm. The antiseptic smell made their nostrils twitch.

"My daughter was like this, once," said the first.

"Kerrigan, you never had a daughter."

"Full well I did," Kerrigan replied. "And for the record, Farad, she was quite the charmer."

"Really? How many men did she ensnare, then? Did she do the rounds?"

Kerrigan turned away from Farad and huffed. "It's not about that."

"The lords would disagree."

"Yes, they would." He reached up to tap his index finger against his cheek. "How was your journey?"

"Cramped. Gates aren't what they used to be."

"And your transition?"

"Ugh." A muscle beneath Farad's eye twitched. "I'm not relishing the return trip."

"We seldom do," Kerrigan sighed. So"

"Her," said Kerrigan.

"Her," Farad agreed. "I'm not in the mood for this."

"You've been wearing the mask too long."

"Yes, well, one can hardly go down the street in broad daylight when they're as ugly as us."

"Ha-ha!" Kerrigan punched Farad's shoulder. "Do you remember Singapore? They thought the world was ending."

"It was, for those fifty in the building," Farad replied, acidly spitting each word. "I don't get how Baskaran and the others enjoy all this.

Kerrigan walked into the room and placed his hand on the girl's forehead. His fingernails were all three inches long. He bent close to the sleeping brunette's face and took a deep sniff through his crooked, pointy nose.

"Business is business," he said.

"Not for me it isn't," Farad replied. He entered the room and parted the blinds. Rain speckled the window. "At least we aren't out in that storm."

Kerrigan joined him at the window. They stared. The monitor continued to blip. He removed from his pocket a golden watch on a golden chain and checked it, tapping at the glass face. Cracks were spreading, their lengthening visible to the eye.

"You or me."

"Oh, for... she's a child!"

"Have you smelt her?" Kerrigan asked. "That's not just antiseptic. Don't you feel it crawling across your skin? It was hard even coming in here with her."

"Like diving into a pool, you know is icy cold," Farad agreed. "My eyes are starting to go." As he said it his pupils flashed red.

"I don't know when it got to this point, but we're here, and the clock is breaking. If we want to win this thing, we have to do it now."

"No witnesses," Farad sighed.

"None," Kerrigan agreed. "I'll do it."

"I'll speak the ritual.

Kerrigan strode across to the girl's side and disconnected the monitor. Farad raised his hands, over which red sparks were dancing. He bared his teeth. His breath hissed out. Kerrigan knelt like a cliff falling into the sea and placed his hand over the girl's heart. His eyes turned white and the traceries of black veins appeared beneath the skin around them.

"Before the light lived the darkness, and the darkness was peace. There was quiet in the black. Then the light blossomed and night was born from day, for before the light there was no night. And then came fire and heat, and the light began to consume the darkness, for cold always falls before heat."

Lines appeared in the air, spiralling above the girl's bed. They cast a pale, jealous luminescence on the walls, and within the swirling symbols were hints of meaning, vapours of almost-comprehension. They whispered, echoing as if in some much larger space.

"Into the light came new life, and the new life had no peace, but was ever restlessly alive, until it returned to darkness. And because the light feared the darkness above all things, it beseeched the Breath giver to aid its survival. To the light was granted the Day bringers - mortals with blazing souls. But the darkness asked for nothing, because all things return to it in time."

Kerrigan closed his eyes and lifted his hand. From the girl's chest rose a star-bright orb that turned the creatures' skin almost translucent, and reveal the twisted skeletons of the beings hidden in those fleshy shells. Farad was shouting now as the whispers rose to a roar, a roar that went unnoticed in the silent corridors of the hospital.

"Because the light's rapacious hunger knew no bounds, the darkness was threatened. But still it asked for nothing, and set its own denizens stirring. And for the first time, those in the darkness were roused to anger. The Scions of Night now drive back the light, that the darkness might not be overcome. Peace will come again."

"For peace, and darkness," Kerrigan grated, his arms starting to smoke from their proximity to the Day sphere.

"Quickly now!"

"Anaiah!"

Kerrigan opened his mouth. His jaw dropped – and kept dropping, widening, expanding, stretching open. He swallowed the orb whole, and for a moment it shone from his pores. Then the creature within him stirred, and clawed hands reached out of his mouth to wrap the orb in shadows. The lines vanished, the glare receded, the roar was silenced. The girl moaned softly.

Kerrigan bent double, holding his chest. Farad lowered his hands.

"The ritual is spoken."

"It never gets any easier," Kerrigan said, his eyes screwed shut.

"Nor should it. We're robbing her of something and she'll never know. Her friends will think she's just become boring. The spring will be gone from her step. Her eyes won't shine anymore." Farad's voice broke. "But we have to! Look at us, Kerrigan. We're in agony because of the Light – because it couldn't leave well alone. Because its very nature destroys us. All we wanted was peace."

"But there was no peace in the Light," Kerrigan finished. "Let's go and have a drink, somewhere."

"I'm sure we can find a place that hasn't paid their electricity bill this month," Farad said, helping his companion up. Kerrigan

reconnected the monitor, which began to repeat its mournful blip. Farad left the room.

Before Kerrigan followed, he paused by the bed and stroked the girl's hand.

"Just like her," he said under his breath, and brushed her hair away from her face. She stirred, mumbled something in her sleep and settled. "No more dreams," he said.

The two creatures walked away down the corridor, each ceiling light dimming as they passed.

During the Halloween season, one popular activity is to visit a haunted house. As a child, some of my earliest and most frightening memories happened in a haunted house at Halloween.

So, let me take you inside a real haunted house. This short story also gives you vocabulary and idioms for describing something scary.We begin as many scary stories have: It is a dark and stormy night.

You walk alone down a desolate street. The rain has been falling steadily all night and is only getting worse. You are soaked to the bone and need to get out of the rain.

Then you see a house. "Thank heavens!" you say out loud. But at second glance, your relief is chilled by the look of the place.

It's dark. Only a lone street lamp casts a dim, yellow light on the sad features of the house. It looks as if no one has lived here for many years. The windows are broken. An old, ripped curtain blows from a third-story window.

Now, you remember where you are. This house is from your childhood. Neighbourhood kids talked of ghosts, from a family long dead, walking through the house at night.

The front yard is tangled with overgrown weeds and vines. A pathway lined with broken stones leads to an old house.

You follow it.

As you walk down the sidewalk, tree branches seem to lean into your path. They grab at your hair and clothes. Spider webs stretched across the branches get caught in your eyes and mouth. As you wipe them away, you hear something behind you.

What is it?! You turn around. Nothing. It was probably just a cat, you tell yourself. Although, you don't believe it.

Just as you step onto the front porch, the door creaks open. Suddenly, two bony hands push you inside. The door slams shut!

From the shadows, things start to come toward you! You can't see anything, but you can hear them coming closer. You run, but running only takes you farther into the nightmare. Your heart beats wildly. Hoping to hide, you open a door, but a skeleton fall into your face. Screaming, you fight with the bones as they entangle your arms and legs! Finally, you break free and run for your life down a hallway.

For a moment, you think you're safe. Then a deathly white hand reaches out from under a table, grabbing at your ankles! You run faster, this time up a flight of stairs. But a half-human, half-bat creature hangs from the ceiling. It flies toward your neck with blood dripping from its razor-sharp teeth.

As you try to escape, you trip down some stairs and fall into a cold, dark basement. From a small window you look outside and see a crazed man holding an axe. He's looking right at you, laughing and seeing you with a scary smile. I should run away and call up someone who can help me. I ran for a while and I found an old house in the jungle and I went inside the old scary house. It was very scary, but I had no choice but to go inside the house to be safe.

I went to in the house and sat at a corner for while and waited until the man got away. It was very dark now outside. I thought that the man had gone and I will go out of the house, but the man was still there outside the house waiting for me to come outside the house. I got really scared and frightened after seeing him standing outside the house for so long in night. Then I got a phone call in the telephone that was kept in the house. Tring.... Tring... I went to the telephone and pick it up and said "hello, whose there..." said politely. I got a replay that you are safe now come out of the house, we have caught the man who was outside the house come and look but she didn't know that the man who was in the call was the man standing outside the house attracting him to come out of the house. He didn't thought about it and said ok I am coming out wait. As he opened the door the man caught him and ran away. The police and the searching team couldn't find the man and him. They only found an axe, shoes and a telephone with a worn piece of cloth. This was still a mystery that where is that man gone...

The end

Contents